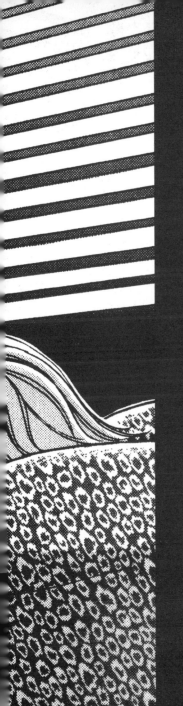

Melanie Schoen
Translation

Miss V
Retouch & Lettering

Topaz Bailey
Design

Michelle Locque
Director of Print Production

Mariko Kumanoya
Publisher

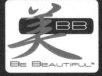

BeBeautifulManga.com

Embracing Love 2. Published by Be Beautiful™, an imprint of A18 Corporation. Office of Publication – 250 West 57th Street, Suite 328, New York, NY 10107. Original Japanese version "Haru wo daiteita Volume 2" © 2000 Youka Nitta. Originally published in Japan in 2000 by Biblos Co., Ltd. English version © 2005 A18 Corporation. Be Beautiful, Original Yaoi and logos are trademarks of A18 Corporation. All rights reserved. Price per copy $15.99, price in Canada may vary. ISBN: 1-933440-03-1.
Catalog #: CMX 69602G. UPC: 8-51988-00103-5-00211.
Printed in Canada

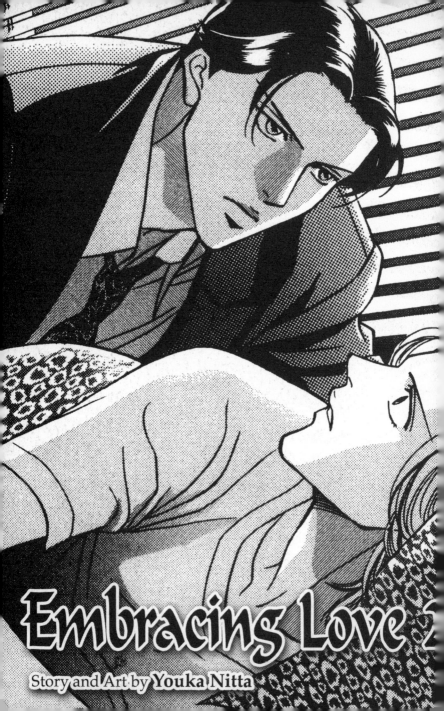

Embracing Love 2

Story and Art by Youka Nitta

CONTENTS

Author's Profile

Youka Nitta

Born March 8th. A Pisces, Blood Type B. I come from Fukui Prefecture, in municipal Tokyo. Writing my profile has been complicated... The truth is, until my third year of high school my blood type was A (according to my maternity record book). It should change again soon... I hope it's AB next...

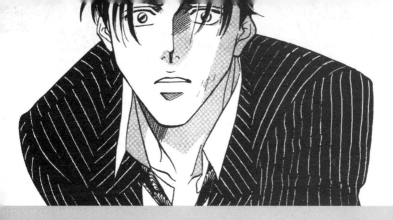

PROFILES

KYOSUKE IWAKI

This ruggedly handsome adult film star's life was turned upside-down when he fell in love with his arch-rival, Katou. The two actors co-starred in a hugely popular TV series called *Embracing Love*, which featured them in a variety of passionate sex scenes with each other. Now, Iwaki struggles with his newfound identity and his feelings for the brash younger man who has pushed him into this strange, new lifestyle.

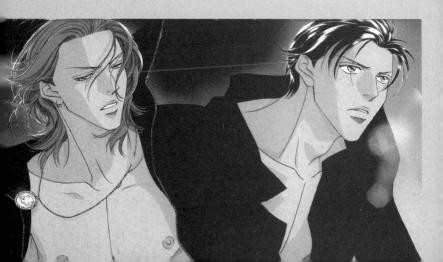

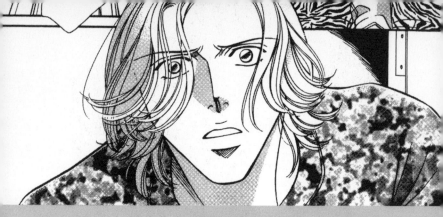

CHARACTER

YOJI KATOU

This beautiful blonde is Iwaki's opposite in every way. Although perfectl content with his life as an adult film star, Katou takes full advantage of th luxuries that mainstream success has afforded him. His passionat feelings for Iwaki seem to know no bounds, and when they're makin love there's nothing he won't do to please his partner. But success has i price, and sometimes it seems that this sensual superstar can't be truste

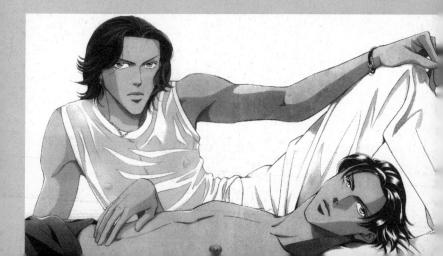

CHARACTER PROFILES

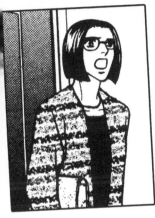

MS. SHIMIZU

Iwaki's personal assistant. She'll go above and beyond the call of duty, especially when Iwaki's heart is broken by one of Katou's scandals.

YOICHI KATOU

Katou's father has difficulty accepting his son's lifestyle, especially when he brings Iwaki to his sister's wedding.

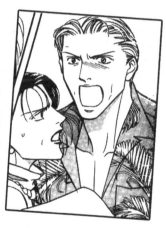

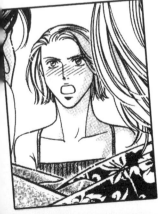

YOUKO KATOU

Katou's sister is a dead ringer for our impossibly beautiful hero, much to the dismay of Iwaki.

CHARACTER PROFILES

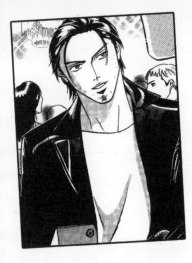

KATSUYA KIKUCHI

Former TV star who was ostracized by a gay scandal ten years ago is now in the midst of a comeback, thanks to the popularity of *Embracing Love*. But rather than enjoying this new opportunity, Kikuchi seethes with jealousy, and looks to drive a wedge between Iwaki and Katou.

KAZUNARI URUSHIZAKI

Freelance photographer bears a striking resemblance to a younger Iwaki, and at one time obsessively stalked Katou. If he appears on the scene, trouble can't be far behind.

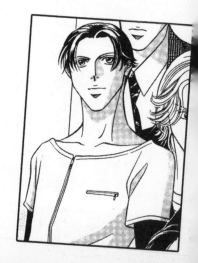

STORY SO FAR

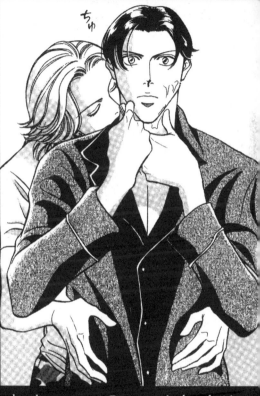

KYOSUKE IWAKI was a popular adult film star, but he'd tired of the endless procession of beautiful women he was forced to make love with. So when he received a mysterious invitation to audition for a film called *Embracing Love*, he jumped at the opportunity. However, he was shocked to discover that his arch-rival, the blonde & beautiful YOJI KATOU, was also up for the role. There was only one thing to do: At the request of the director, the cross-dressing NAGISA SAWA, the two actors performed a passionate sex scene in order to win the coveted role. Iwaki won the part, as well as the affections of Katou.

Embracing Love was a huge hit, so Sawa created a television series as a vehicle to pair Iwaki and Katou. It was a mixed blessing for Iwaki, who was pleased to have mainstream success, but was unhappy with being perceived as gay. Katou had no such problems, and relished his passionate sex scenes with Iwaki.

But nothing good lasts forever, and soon *Embracing Love* wrapped for the season. Concerned that he'd never see his paramour again, Katou bribed Iwaki's landlord and had his belongings moved into Iwaki's apartment. Now they'll be together all the time, and Iwaki is left to wonder if that's truly a good thing.

Which brings us to the next chapter of our story…

Selfish Gene
セルフィッシュ・ジーン
利己的遺伝子

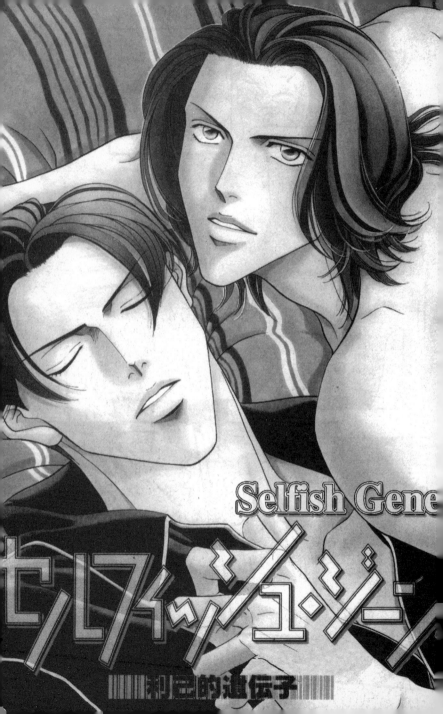

STEP
ヒ…
SLIDE
ス…

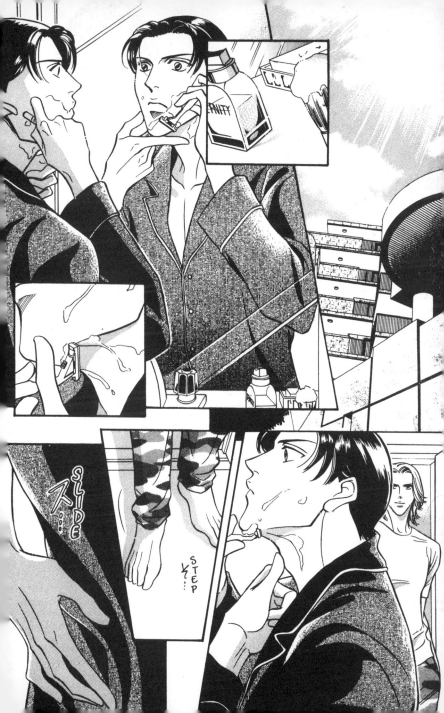

KISS ちゅ
Good morning, Iwaki-san. ♡
You--
Idiot!
Ah… あ…
STING スゥ…

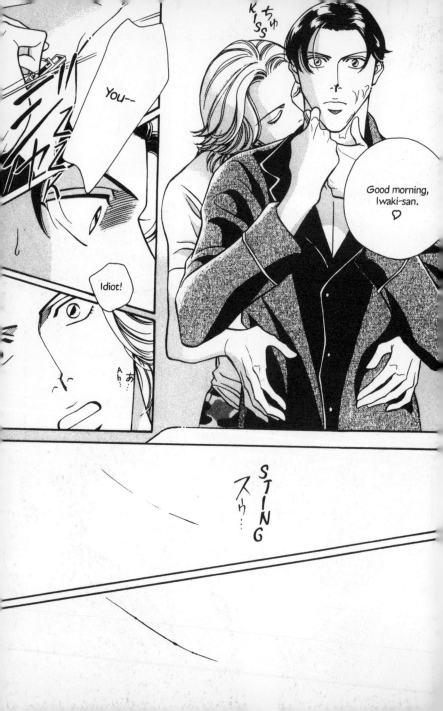

ぶるぶる
QUIVER QUIVER
You idiot, Katou!
I'm sorry, I'm sorry!
What happened to you, Iwaki!? What's with the bandage!?

Today is your big interview for the new show! Can't you get rid of it?
I can't. It's pretty deep...I'm sorry.
But you're usually so careful. What happened?
REJECTED
I'm so sorry, **Ms. Shimizu.** He was shaving, and I grabbed him...
WHACK
...and, well...
Ow! That hurt, Iwaki-san! You're awful.
Forget about him. Let's get going.
HEH HEH HEH HEH

Iwaki-san! Don't forget, I'll have dinner waiting for you tonight! Hurry back!
That idiot.
He didn't have to shout it.
GIGGLE
くすくす
You certainly have yourself an adorable wife, Mr. Iwaki.
UGH
げそ…
...Give me a break.
Not you, too, Shimizu.

RATTLE
By the way, not to butt in...
...But please keep your relationships limited to Mr. Katou.
Always remember that the media is keeping an eye on you.
Your public likes you and Katou together. We don't want to risk your popularity with any kind of scandal.
That sort of thing could ruin your image.
-Sigh-
...I understand, Ms. Shimizu.
It's been a month since Katou moved himself in.
And gradually, I've come to feel like I'm suffocating.

MURMUR
Okay folks, here are the **first** scenes for our new drama, *Selfish Gene.* Take one copy and pass the rest around.
Let's begin by introducing the cast.
Since the apartment only has one bedroom, Katou's claimed the living room for himself.
He meddles with me every time he sees me. My private life is completely disrupted.
The crazy thing is, he hasn't really tried to get us to sleep together. What could he be thinking?
STAND
HUH?
CLAP CLAP
Everyone, this is our lead, **Mr. Kyosuke Iwaki.** He'll be playing the role of *Naoki Ishii,* whose ex-wife has forced their kids on him.
CLAP CLAP
And playing the role of *Nami Morimoto,* the student who falls in love with him, is **Ms. Ryoko Suehiro.**
CLAP CLAP
Thank you very much.

MURMUR
Good to meet you, Mr. Iwaki.
I used to watch *Embracing Love* every day.
SLIDE
MURMURMUR
May I ask you about your bandage? Are you maybe hiding a **hickey?**
From Katou, maybe?
BLUSH
It's not **like** that! I cut myself **shaving**!!
Really? That doesn't quite fit your image. It's still cute, though.
Will you be attending tonight's staff party? I'd like to talk with you some more.
Hurry back!
I'll have dinner waiting!

Of **course** I'll come.
There's no need to worry. It's not like he's really my lover. He always imposes himself on me at his convenience.
Selfish Gene... It's as if this phrase was coined just for him.

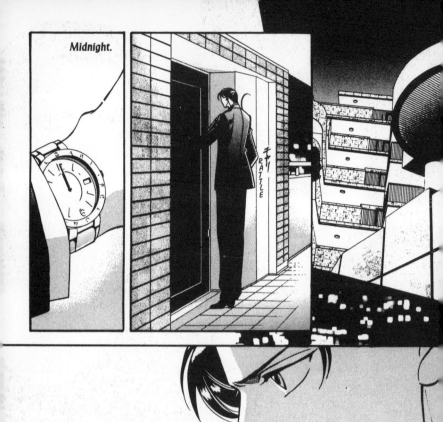

Midnight.

RATTLE

When I was living alone, I wouldn't care about coming back this late.

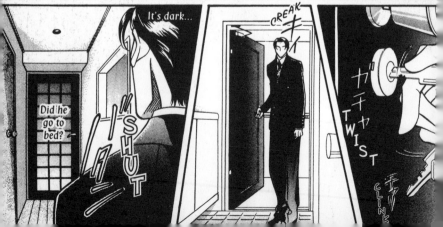

It's dark...

Did he go to bed?

CREAK

SHUT

TWIST

CLINK

カチャ
K-CHA
キシ…
CREAK
waki-san
have to get up early
tomorrow, so I went to
bed. Sorry if I make
too much noise in the
morning.
-Katou

THTHUMP
ズキ…
CREAK
ギシ…
…

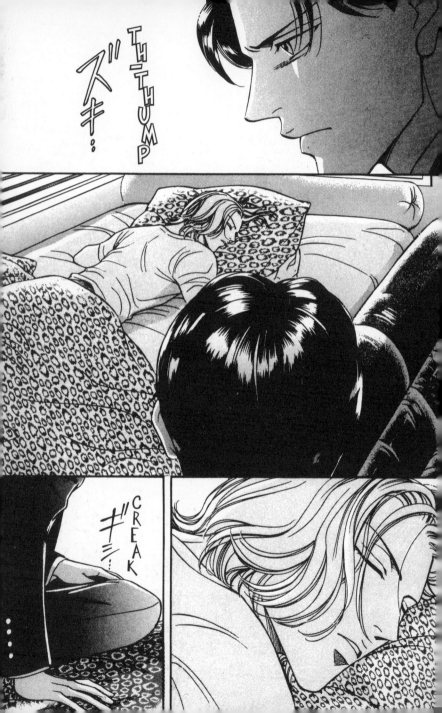

Thierry Mugler
I've had to restrain myself ever since he came into my life.
In my relationships...
n my work...
Even my private life...
And all because he's so selfish...
Everything goes at his pace...

ギシ…
SHIFT
So why am I the only one who...?
Mm...

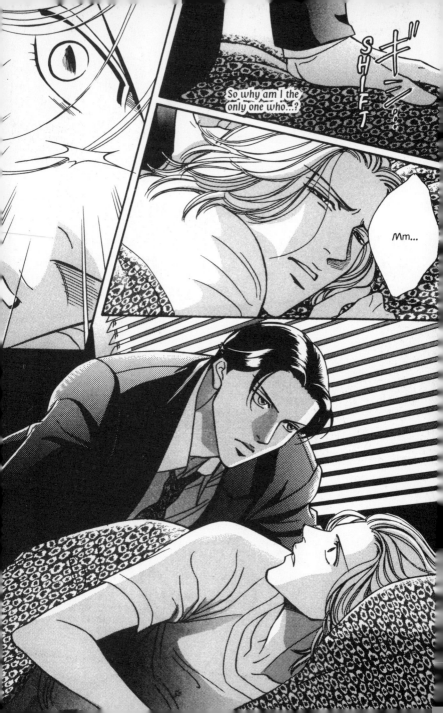

.....
Welcome back, Iwaki-san. You gonna make love to me now?
ギッ GRAB
What happened to you? **Seriously.** I won't be mad.
Shut up. I'm not moving at **your** pace anymore...

Well, okay, Iwaki-san. Since you're willing.
SHIVER

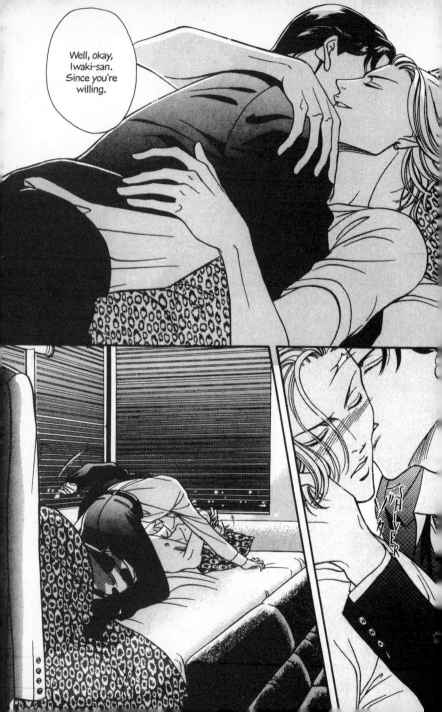

Iwaki-san...
"Being made love to" by someone you love doesn't just feel good...it's so much more.
I hope you feel that way too... sometime soon.

.....
What is it Iwaki-san? Go ahead... It's okay.
Ah...
I...!
Is this **really** okay...?

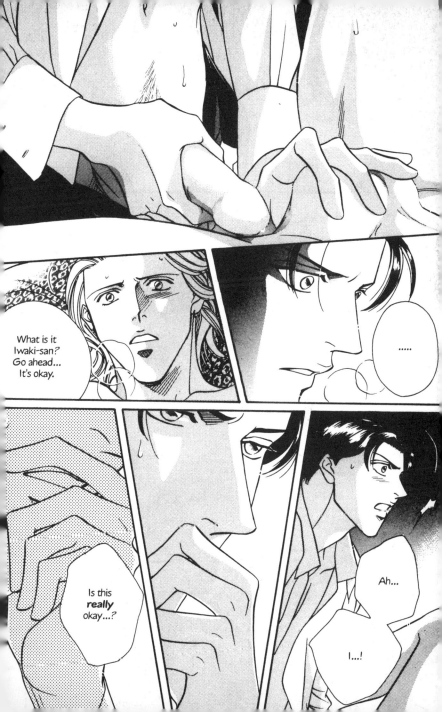

...You...
You always... do me.
Huh?
If...you'd rather do it **that** way, you just have to **say** so. I...don't care.
.....
!?
YANK
くしゃ くしゃ
RUSTLE
SIGH

That's not **really** it...is it, Iwaki-san?
You just don't like the idea that **doing me** might make you accept my **feelings** for you.

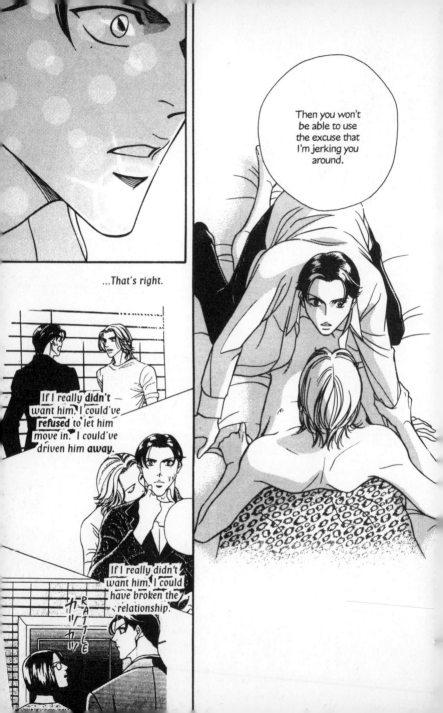

Then you won't be able to use the excuse that I'm jerking you around.

...That's right.

If I really **didn't** want him, I could've **refused** to let him move in. I could've driven him **away**.

If I really didn't want him, I could have broken the relationship.

I had so **many** chances...
SMIRK
Just kidding. Was I too harsh?
Kind of pushy of me when I moved in uninvited.
Sorry. I'll make you feel really good to make up for it.
I've been acting like the victim...
But **I'm** the one that's been selfish...

WAVER
ユサ
WAVER
ユサ
GRAB
ぎゅ…
Katou...
...I'm sorry.
...Iwaki-san?
I **blamed** so many things on you...
I...I'm **sorry.**

It's okay, Iwaki-san.
You didn't do it to me...
...Because you'd feel **bad** for me if your feelings weren't ***genuine.***
That means you understand my ***sincerity.***
It's that ***serious*** side of you that I love, Iwaki-san.

FOOMP
Someday.. Maybe not today...
But someday... that serious Iwaki-san will truly accept me.
You can... do it to me...
He understands me...
He really understands me.
My good points and my bad points.

He accepts me more honestly than anyone ever has.
Nn!?
Iwaki-san, I'm sorry!!
THRUST
THWAP
But...But I can't hold back!!
HWAP

SMACK
Nn... Nn... NNN!!
SMACK
Ohhh, Katou...!
SMACK
SMACK
I'm...I'm gonna... *I'm gonna...*
It's exactly as Katou said.
It's not just pleasure...

HAA
HAA
!?
WINCE

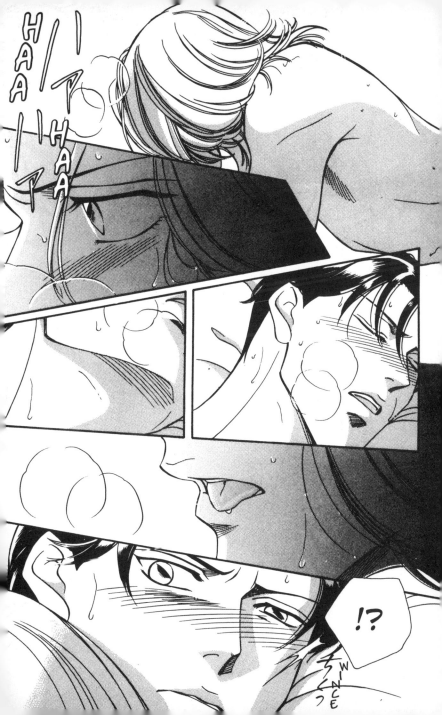

KISS
Your scratch from this morning...
I can still taste a little blood left.
I feel like I'm beginning to understand.

Katou...can I ask you something?
Hm? Yes, of **course.**
Why didn't you lay a hand on me all month?
You won't get mad?
I don't know. **Should** I?

FLOP
PEEK
TUR
I wanted... *I thought...* I'd get to see you... **masturbate.**
STARTLE
What!?
Ee!!
Come on, it was just a little joke...I was having **fun**! Isn't that the best part of living together!?
I thought that if I got you really **hot** but didn't follow through with anything that you'd...well, **you** know!

Get out of my bed!!
....
I'm sorry, Iwaki-san! I'm sorry!!
And just when we were starting to have a nice atmosphere together.
Selfish Gene / END

109
GIGOLO POUR HOMME
So did you get that poster? The one of Katou in the Gigolo perfume ad?
Yeah! I went to the train station early this morning, but all that was left were the perfume posters.
ワンナイト・ジゴロ
ONE NIGHT GIGOLO
So I bought the perfume and forced it on my boyfriend.
Now he can wear it during sex and I'll pretend Katou's making love to me. It's *so* cool.
Really? You're evil!

ワンナイト・ジゴロ
ONE NIGHT GIGOLO

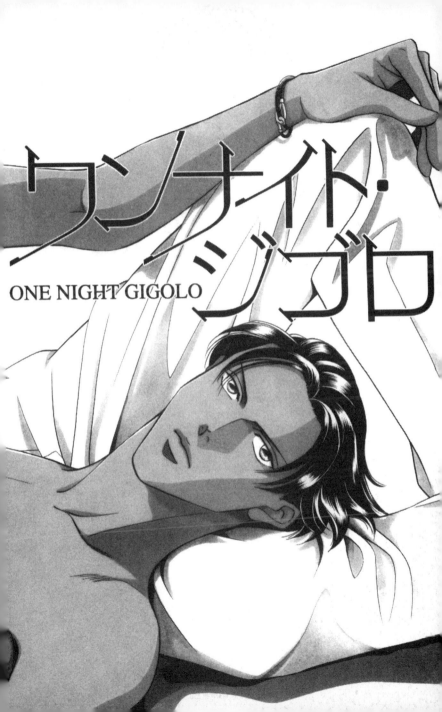

A scent you remember only between the sheets
FLIP
FLIP
FLIP
500 women surveyed
Ranking of men that women want to sleep with
1 Yoji Katou
2 Takashi Takenouchi
3 Toshiaki Hakamada
4 TELU
5 Takeshi Inada
6 Kyosuke Iwaki

Hello? I'm home!
FLIP
FLIP
K-CHA
カチャ
Ah!
FLOP
Oh, Iwaki-san. I'm *so* tired!
I've been so **busy** lately, and it's so lonely not seeing you every day!
HMPH

Are you wearing "Gigolo?"
Oh, you noticed! I have a bunch, so I'll give you some.
We can frame it, if you want.
STAND
?
Hey, now that I think about it, aren't **you** posing for the new *Selfish Gene* poster tomorrow?
I'll be at studio right next door, shooting the next *Gigolo* poster. We could go together!
K-CHAK
カチャ
....

SLAM
?
an·an

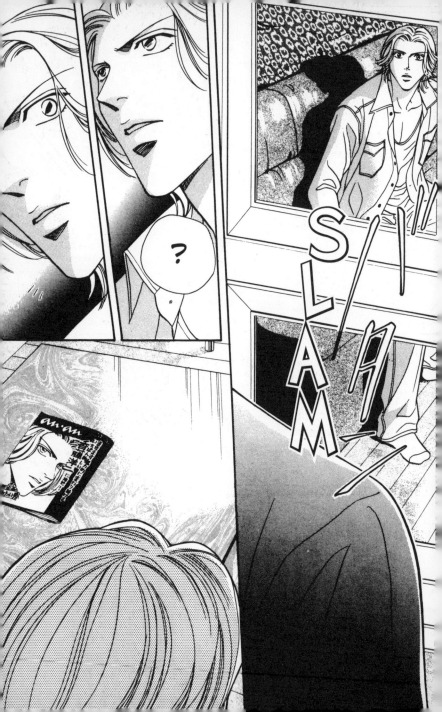

SIGH ふぅ
...Not again...
6 Kyosuke Iwaki
7 Toshiaki
AOYAMA STUDIO
Good work today, Mr. Iwaki. Your best, **ever**!

カツ STEP
カツ STEP
カツ STEP
カツ STEP
GRAB
Come here for a second, Iwaki-san.

FLASH
STEP
STEP
STEP
Let go of me, Katou! I said...STOP!
STEP
STEP
STEP
If you want to talk, it can wait until we get home. I'm on a schedule, here.
What are you talking about? Your next shoot isn't for hours, yet!

We're completely alone, here. No one can see us...or hear us.
Now tell me why you've been **avoiding** me.
I haven't been...
Yes, you have!! You left this morning as **soon** as you could!
And when I asked if we could go together you **ignored** me!!
You're bothered by that stupid article, aren't you?

Stupid article?
That's just feedback from a small group of women.
It's not fair to take it out on me.
There's nothing I can do about that!
And now you're **ignoring** me over this stupid thing? I can't ***stand*** it!
?

What are you talking about, Katou?
Huh?
You mean, you're **not** mad about losing to me in the *"Men That Women Want"* ranking?
Then **why** are you in such a bad mood? Did I **do** something?
Damn. I should've blamed the magazine. What'll I say, **now?**

Relax, Katou. This is all just your **imagination.**
It's not that I was **bothered** by the article, I was just **amazed** there were so many women wanting to sleep with you.
Thanks to *Gigolo,* you have a chance to change your "gay" image.
So maybe you should stop chasing a guy like me.
....
Huh...?

I don't believe it Iwaki...
You're actually jealous...?
I know what you're saying...
You're upset that millions of women want to sleep with me... not for losing in the ranking.
Shut up!! That's not wha I'm saying!!
Uh...

That's it, **isn't** it, Iwaki-san?
That makes me... dangerously happy.
ちゅっ KISS
ちゅっ KISS
Ohhhh...
Katou...

KISS
ちゅ…
Hey, Iwaki-san. Do you think I've become... **perverted** since falling for you?
Being with you...making love to you... I have bad thoughts every day.
You're already a pervert, Katou.
Oh, Iwaki-san. Listen to me...
Y'know, *Gigolo* isn't exactly my favorite scent...
But when I saw the sales message I decided on something and... decided to wear it every day...

The next day we're both off, I want to spend a **whole day** making love with you.
Until my smell is in every nook and cranny of your skin, and we can't even get off the bed.
I must be dumb, thinking about stuff like that so seriously.

ごくっ…
GULP
I have to tell this idiot to stop dreaming! Not to get carried away!!
Katou, I...I have to ask...
What? Ask me **anything**!
When you fall for someone...does everyone become as **stupid** as you?
Do you think I'm stupid, Iwaki-san? Is **that** it? Don't **say** that...Even my feelings can get hurt.

Answer me, Katou! Will I... become stupid, too?
I...I don't...
What am I saying...? This is dumb!
Forget it! Forget I said anything!!

Have you... never been in love?
BLUSH
Only with women!!
I don't just mean dating. True love has nothing to do with gender.
Don't spout your senseless theories at me, Katou!
How interesting. Even though you were such a cool porno star...
I see...So now that you're falling for me, I've become your first love. My heart is pounding.
Don't talk over me!! Listen to me!!

I'm coming to understand your stubbornness, Iwaki-san.
A man like you who is so afraid of love...might be just right becoming 'stupid.'
I want to watch you as you soften.
I'll definitely make you fall for me.

Not now, Katou. You still have work...!
FLINCH
Heh.
Too late. I've already been carried away by the mood.
So help me unwind, okay?
After all, I can't go back to work all hard like this...
...Even if it is an ad for Gigolo. I can't overdo it...Gotta keep the sponsors happy, y'know.

SLIDE
Do you have a handkerchief, Iwaki-san?
I'm wearing these clothes for the shoot, so they can't get...**dirty.**
Yeah...In my pocket.
Good.
THAP
THAP

MMM
Ahh...
Just like that, Iwaki-san... Yesss...
Faster.
KISS
Nn...!
Ohhhhh.

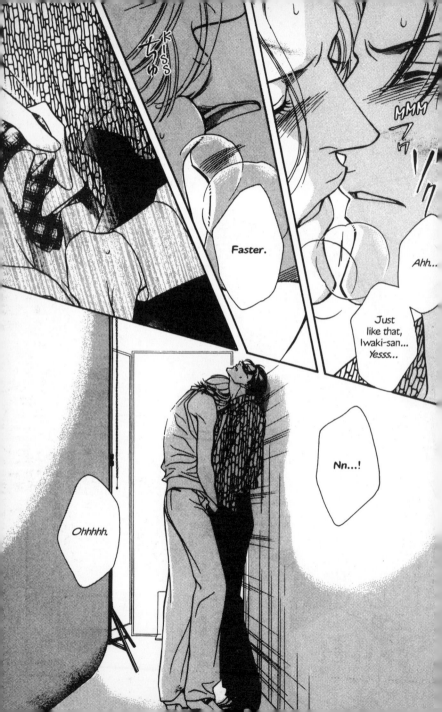

Thank you, Iwaki-san.
HUFF HUFF
HUFF HUFF
SLAM
CLANG
Our model just did WHAT?!?
STEP STEP
...In a car accident. The model's unhurt, but traffic will be delayed for **hours**!
But that's no excuse for ruining Mr. Katou's schedule! Find a **replacement**!!
Damn...!
On such short notice!? We'll **never** find someone in time!
ZIP

Whisper
Iwaki-san, hide for a second!
HAAH
HAAH
Hi, fellas. What's going on?
Mr. Katou!?
I was taking a nap backstage when I heard the noise.
Is there some kind of trouble?
Yes, there is. I'm so sorry.

Your co-star can't make it...
...And we're looking for a **replacement** right now.
FLINCH
But aren't we working **nude** today? You won't find someone too easily.
STEP
Excuse me, but perhaps...I can help?
Mr. Iwaki!?

What's Mr. Iwaki doing here?
Sir!!
Isn't it obvious!?
Whisper
Iwaki-san, why did you come out?
Not that I mind.
You're looking for a model, right?
Well...yes, we are...
....

But...Iwaki-san was so concerned about his image...
Could it be that he's jealous?
Could it be...he doesn't want more women around me?

He's not aware of his own feelings...
He's adorable!!
Well gents, since he's already **here** and everything, let's **do it**!
Well, since Mr. Katou says it's okay...
Let's get everything ready.

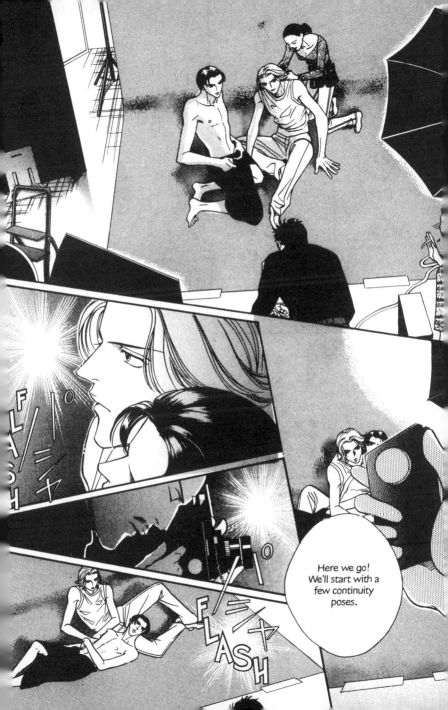

Here we go!
We'll start with a
few continuity
poses.

WHISPER
Sir...Mr. Iwaki has some impressive expressions.
That's terrific! Just like that! Pose more seductively... Yes! Just like that!

WIDE
The new poster for *Gigolo* is stopping people in their tracks. It's quite the hot topic.
Yoji Katou is back, but **this** time he's paired with his real life lover, Kyosuke Iwaki.
It's causing quite a stir! Rumors are flying!
Although Mr. Iwaki was not the producers' first choice...
...The sponsors loved his test shots and selected him for the promotion.
Chatter chatter
Here's some opinions from the streets. *"Wow, it's really cool."*
I like it better than the last one.
"Of course I like Katou, but Iwaki is beautiful, too."
Ha ha ha! "Beautiful?"
Chatter chatter
"Anyone who didn't like Iwaki before should see this!"
I know, I know!

ROMEO GIGL
Think they're **overdoing** a good thing?
HEH
If you think so, don't happily hang that poster in the living room.

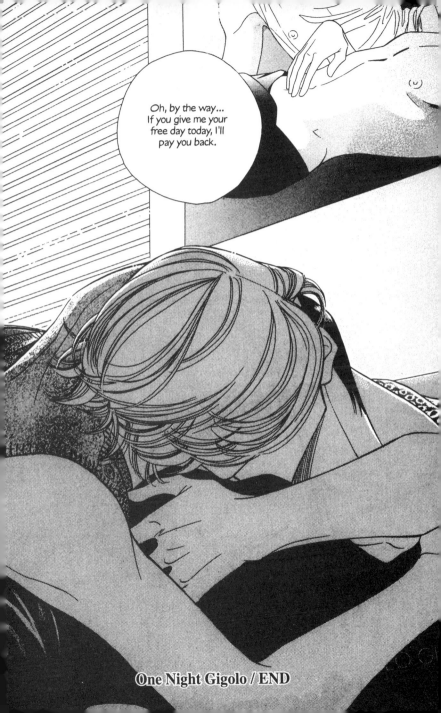

Oh, by the way...
If you give me your
free day today, I'll
pay you back.

One Night Gigolo / END

ファミリーツリー
Family Tree

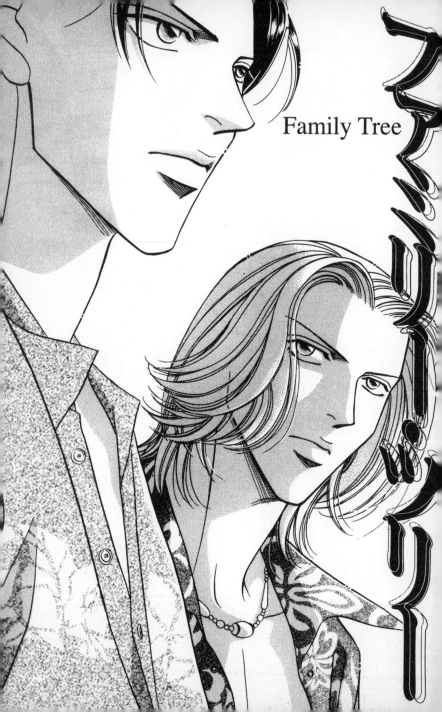

Good work today, Mr. Iwaki!
I'll pick you up at 10AM tomorrow.
GCHAK
Thanks again. Goodnight.
VROOM
BEEP
BEEP
Iwaki-san!!

VROOM
Oh. Hi, Katou...
Situations like this really make it feel like we're living together!!
CLICK
You've been ridiculously **cheery** lately, you know.
Don't say "living together." It sounds weird.
Iwaki
Katou
岩城
香藤
DDI

Here. It's for you.
Really? For me?
It's from my little sister.
I wonder what it is...
How rare.
RIP
ear Brother,
veryone in the family
s relieved that your
vork is going well. I
now this is sudden, but
have to tell you. I'm
etting married! The
eremony's being held
n Hawaii, so you won't
ave to worry about the
nedia, either. I've
vritten the date down
or you, so please find a
vay to get out of work
o you can attend. Call
ne when you can,
kay?
-Yoko

Married!?
カチ CLICK
ウィー UMMMMMM
She's having the ceremony in Hawaii, because there won't be any media concerns for me.
But I know *she's* always wanted to marry in Hawaii!
...So you still hear from your family?
ウィー UMMMMMM

Not after becoming a world renowned porno star, I don't.
Huh... You don't?
I did hear from them after *Embracing Love* came out...
...But nothing else after the scandal with you went public.
Ah...
AH
チーン! BLING
I'm sorry. It's my fault...
ポ PET
ガー SLIDE
Don't worry about it.
If **they** won't talk to me... because of **this**... then who needs them?

I know!! Will you come to the ceremony with me!?
Huh!?
Don't be stupid!! A stranger like me can't just show up at a wedding!!
Your parents would **never** allow it!!
It's okay! My family's **open** about stuff like that. And if you're my **lover**, you're **not** a stranger.
Heck, they even accepted my porn career!

I'm **sure** my family will be **thrilled**! We'll keep it all a secret and **surprise** them!! Okay!?
Hn...
I'm not so sure I should be giving in to Katou like this...
Hawaii, six months later.

Go home!!
Huh...?
What!?
What the hell, Dad!? That's a **terrible** attitude to give Iwaki-san after he came all the way here!
Yoji, stop this!
CLATTER
Well, I never asked **either** of you to come!!

Are you trying to make a **mockery** of your sister's wedding, Yoji!?
What will the groom's parents think when they see the bride's brother and his male lover!?
I don't care what you're doing back in Japan...and I don't want to know, either! If word of your **wicked ways** were to get out, I wouldn't be able to walk the streets again!
That's how it is!! Don't involve your family with your lifestyle!

SSSHH
....
I'm sorry.
SPLASH
Why are **you** apologizing!?

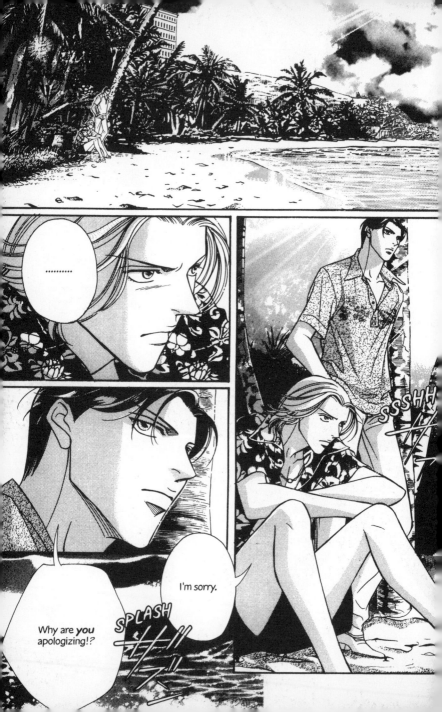

I'm pissed at my father for embarrassing me in front of the man I love...
...and I'm pissed at **myself** for thinking he was such an **understanding** man!
I'm not surprised he was upset, Katou. This was a **stupid** idea, coming here like this.
Asking your father to accept the fact that you love another man is a **lot** to ask for.
You should be grateful he accepts you at all! Don't push him away.
Please try to under-stand...
Won't you go apologize? He won't want to see me.
Why bother!! And I'm not going to the ceremony, either!
Let's just pack our bags and get the hell out of here!

Don't be such a child!!
There's no point in being cold to your family! If you just **compromise** a bit, then none of you have to suffer!
But if I do **that,** Iwaki-san...then **you're** the one that'll be hurt!!
I felt awful when you told me about your family.
I wanted to introduce you to my family so that you'd feel more at home!!
And now it's all a **mess**!!
ふぅ SIGH
I assumed it was our ages that made us think differently...but you really **are** a child.
Katou...

Why didn't you think it would upset me to see your happy family?
I...
PAT
But I knew you were thinking of me when you invited me here.
So I came. I was happy hat you were hinking of me.

So don't just worry about me.
Think about how your **family** feels, too.
Okay?
You really do seem very **mature** sometimes, Iwaki-san...
...Even if you're usually just cute.
Heh.
You're the only one that thinks that.

Iwaki-san... I've always wanted to ask you this...
I know nothing about you...
You said you left home for acting. So where are you from?
Niigata. You shouldn't ave been afraid o ask. Both my parents are well.
I have an older brother, too.
Really? I always figured you'd be the oldest. Do you look like him?
Not really...but we have similar features.
He's bigger boned. He's a straight-laced public official, totally different from me.

It's not all that interesting, really.
What about you? I didn't see your sister today--do **you** look alike?
Snicker
Laughably so.
Yeah...? If she looks like you, she must be pretty cute...
Not reall
Maybe a little...
Huh!?

SNICKER
くすくす
What?
What am I going to do with him?
All right, Iwaki-san. I'll go to the ceremony.
I'll do it for my sister, who's "cute like me."

Idiot, I didn't mean it like that!
Then how did you mean it?
Uh...!
Anyone who heard you would have thought the same.
You think I'm cute...

What are you doing? We can't...not out here!
Let anyone come! They can't stop us!
Nnn!
You don't want to stop, either...!
It's not fair to always make **me** out as the selfish one.

....
I don't dislike having sex with you...
Really!?
But...I'm not like you...I can't do it in public.
I worry about being seen...
Okay!!

I can't believe you said that.
It's the **first** time you've said you like having sex with me!
ちゅ… KISS
ピクッ FLINCH
You've been spoiling me lately, Iwaki-san.
And now, I'm happy...
I'm so very happy that it's scary.

ちゅ…
KISS
しゅ…
SLIDE
KISS
ちゅ
Ahhh...

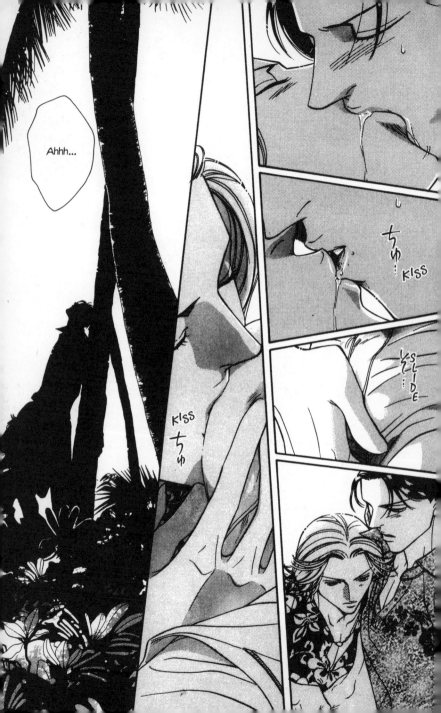

Ah... ahh... yes!
Katou...
SLURP
Lift your legs higher, Iwaki-san... like that.
THRUST
Mnn!!

SHUDDER
Nn...nn...
Nnn...!
SHUDDER
THAP
THAP
Ah... ah...
SQUISH
SQUISH
Ka...tou... nnn...

...Hey...
Iwaki-san...
I know I might seem like a kid, sometimes...
And maybe I spend so much time **dreaming** that I don't know when to accept the truth.
But if nothing else, believe this...
I'm always prepared to accept your joy **and** sorrow!

I'll always be your family...
SPLASH

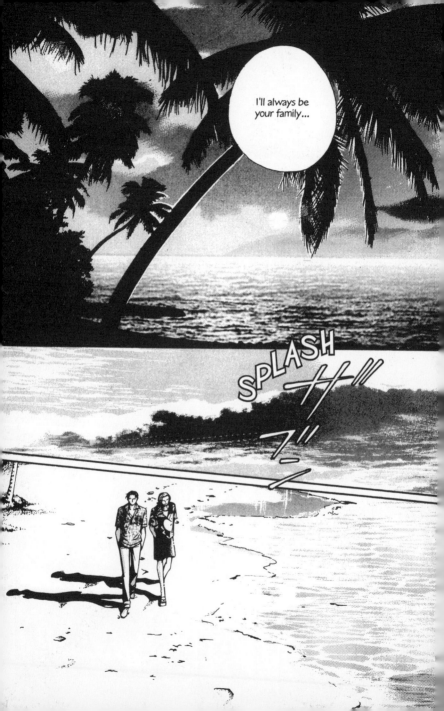

Brother!
Youko?
That's your sister? You really **do** look alike.
See?
It's really obvious.

You're Mr. Iwak right?
Nice to meet you. I'm Youko. Thanks for looking after my brother.
Nice to meet you, too.
This is a little strange.
I'm so sorry my father was rude to you!!
Please come to the ceremony together, both of you!!
It's **my** wedding so my parents can't complain! My fiancé agrees!
And, Mr. Iwaki...

Whatever my father says, my brother chose you.
Man or woman, you're not a stranger!! I want you to celebrate with us.
Well said, Sister!
Looks like it's not just your face that's laughably similar.
Yeah, really.

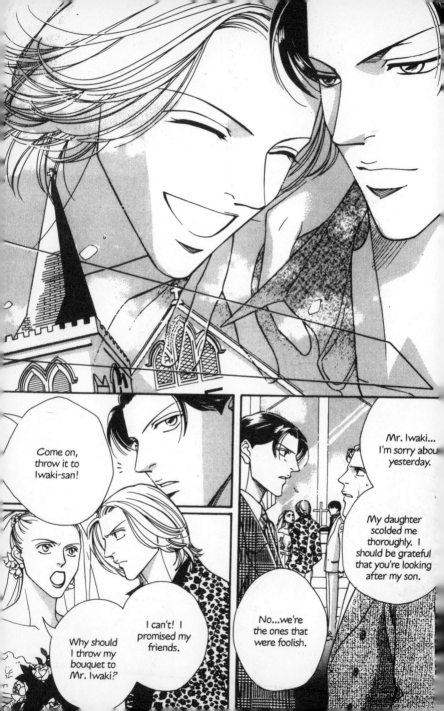

Come on, throw it to Iwaki-san!

Why should I throw my bouquet to Mr. Iwaki?

I can't! I promised my friends.

No...we're the ones that were foolish.

Mr. Iwaki... I'm sorry abou yesterday.

My daughter scolded me thoroughly. I should be grateful that you're looking after my son.

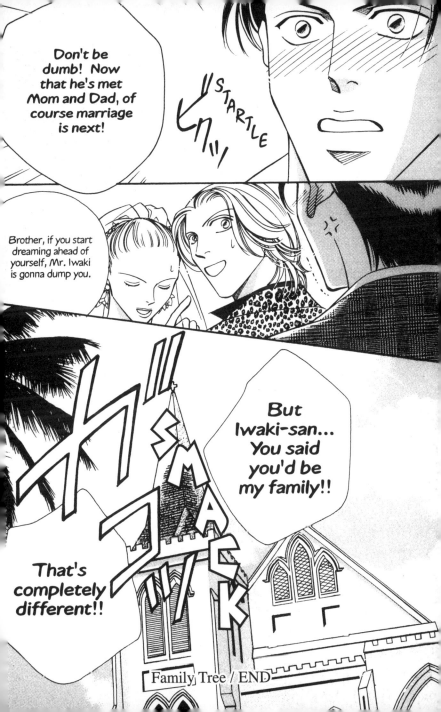

Don't be dumb! Now that he's met Mom and Dad, of course marriage is next!

STARTLE

Brother, if you start dreaming ahead of yourself, Mr. Iwaki is gonna dump you.

But Iwaki-san... You said you'd be my family!!

That's completely different!!

Family Tree / END

Reason for Living
レーゾン・デートル
RAISON D'ÊTRE

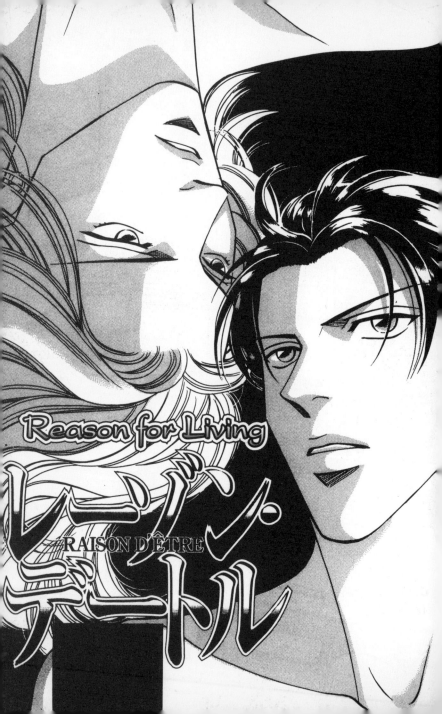

RING
トゥルルル
トゥルルル
RING
Hello, this is Iwaki.
Oh, good morning Ms. Shimizu.
Really? I'm leaving right now.
CLICK
SHUT
25
K
Overseas Interview
I
Fuchu Studio 7:00
There he is!!

FLASH
FLASH
FLASH
Mr. Iwa what ar your feelings
Mr. Iwaki, what are your thoughts about this new article!?
FLAS
What in the world is this...!!
Don't you know!?
THE WIDE

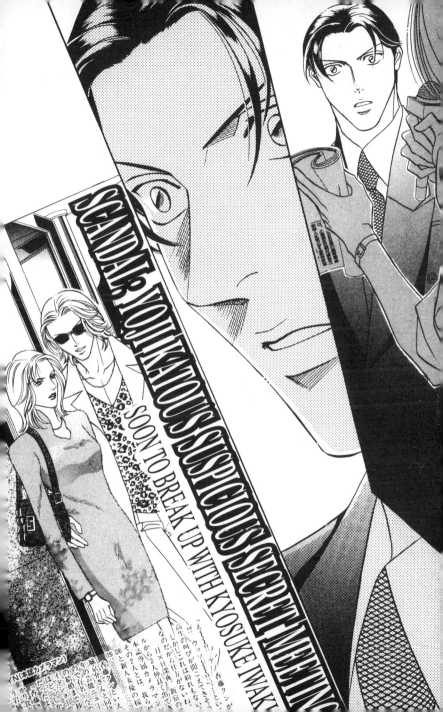

SCANDAL! YOJI KATOU'S SUSPICIOUS SECRET MEETING!

SOON TO BREAK UP WITH KYOSUKE IWAK...

Mr. Iwaki, do you know this mystery blonde!?
FLASH
Mr. Iwaki!!
How has Mr. Katou's betrayal effected your love life!?
FLASH
Iwaki was speechless when confronted with the news of Mr. Katou's infidelity.
Mr. Katou is working overseas on a photo campaign scheduled to debut this winter, and could not be reached for comment.
THE WIDE
Infidelity Revealed!?
Kyosuke Iwaki and Yoji Katou
A-BREAKUP?!
So for the moment, all the attention has concentrated on Mr. Iwaki.
Cut!

What's wrong, Iwaki? You're not paying attention to your lines!!
I know your private life is a mess, but pull yourself together!!
I'm sorry...
This isn't like you, Iwaki.
You look awful.
Have you decided how you'll respond to that article?
Look, what Katou did was pretty cruel, huh? Well, I never thought it'd last forever.
We're going to move ahead, so standby for scene 11...
Mr. Iwaki...?
Excuse me. I'm going to the roof for some air. I need to be alone.

プァッ BEEP
プァ BEEP
CHT カチ
FUUUU フゥ
I knew it...

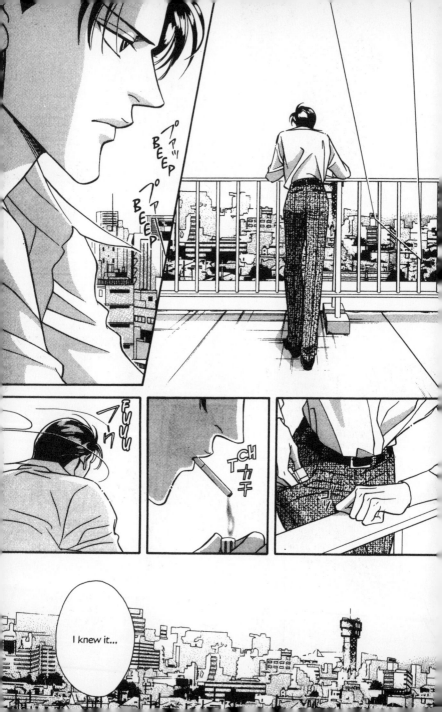

I knew the day would come when he changed his mind, and turned his eyes to another.
That's why I tried to never fully believe his words.
QUIVER
It was pissing me off.
Vatching you do
with that guy...

I don't want this feeling to end!
Is it just going to fade away? Huh, Iwaki-san!?
I'll always be your family...
DRIP ポタ...
DRIP ポタ...
Why did he say all those things...if he was only going to change his mind?
Nn... unn...

How did it come to this?
Mn...
unn...
VROOOM

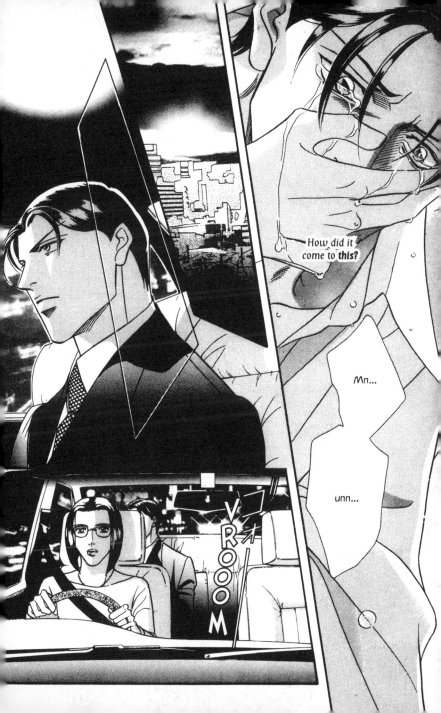

RING RING
VROOM
CLICK
Hello, it's Shimizu.
Huh!? Mr. Katou?
FLINCH
Mr. Iwaki, it's Mr. Katou for you.
....

I'm sorry, but Mr. Iwaki is tied up at the moment.
Yes...yes.
I understand. I'll tell him.
VROOOOOM
Mr. Katou has just arrived in Narita.
He was surprised by the commotion that's been going on here.
He says at article as entirely nade up.
But because the press is swarming he won't be able to get home tonight.
....
Um...
The media is probably still flooding the area around your apartment. Should I arrange for a hotel?
Please do...

カチャ
K-CHA
ドサ
FLOP
So tired...

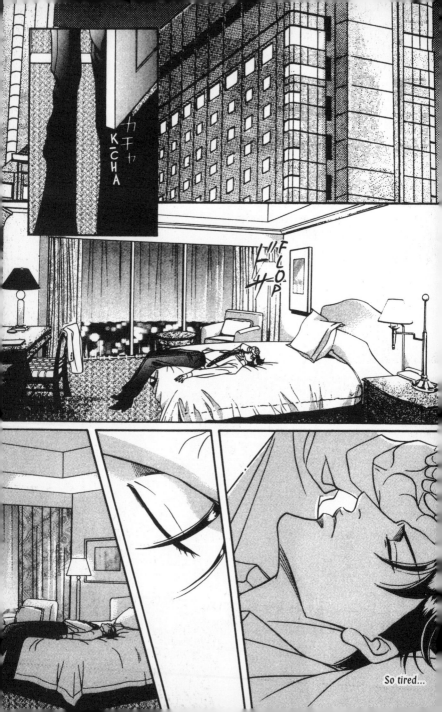

KNOCK KNOCK
KNOCK KNOCK
STEP
K-CHA
Katou...!
Let me in, Iwaki-san.
Please... **listen** to what I have to say.

....
K-CHAK カチャ
I'm sorry... forcing my way in on top of all the other trouble I've caused.
But I didn't think you'd let me in otherwise.
Shimizu told me you were here... But I made her, so don't be angry with her.
It's not the **first** time you two have worked together.

That's... true, but...
You're... angry, aren't you?
I said on the phone that was all a **big lie**!!
I wasn't alone with that woman-- we were with a huge group of friends!! The photographer cropped them out of the shot!
You're the **only** one I love, Iwaki-san!!

....
Even now...all you make are **excuses.**
Tell me you changed your mind and I'll understand.
It's not like I've **believed** your lies before.
What...?

Why are you taking everything back all of a sudden!? You **always** try to do that!
Shimizu told me you were falling apart today!!
You **do** believe in me! That's why it was such a **shock** to you, right!?
Believe me, Iwaki-san!! I don't care what **anyone** else says, as long as **you** believe me!!

I don't want to get jerked around by you.
...I don't want to get hurt again.
Katou!?
FWOOMP

I **will** hurt you, over and over...
...If it proves that you really do love me!
I'll jerk you around...I'll do whatever it takes... but I'll never let you run away!!
RIP
Stop it, Katou!!
No...I won't.

Not if you really believe...
...The lies in that article more than me!
!!
...Could it be?
If Katou is going this far, maybe that article really was a fake.
He's not the kind o man to lie like tha But that isn't what hurting me.
...I'm beginning to realize...how deeply he is in my heart.

If I let him any deeper...
When the day comes when he really does leave me... I will completely fall apart.
So you're not going to **say** anything...You're just going to let me **do** you?
You won't even moan...are you rejecting me?
...!!

I said I wouldn't let you run away, right...?
YANK
THRUST
......!!
~~~!!
~~~

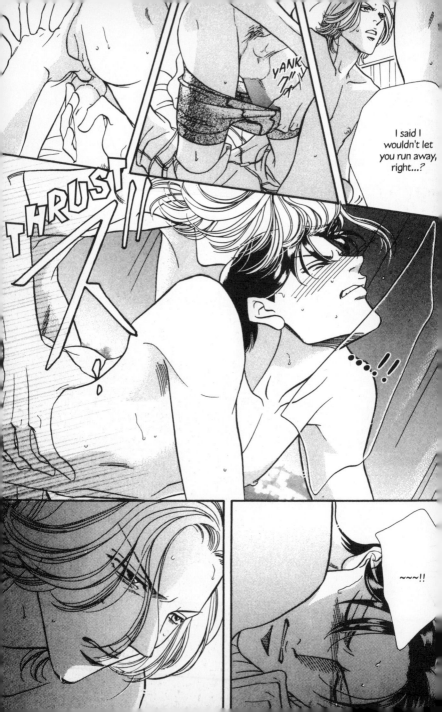

Call out for me... Iwaki-san...
SHUDDER
...Nn...
Call my name like you always do...
Please...

Iwaki-san...

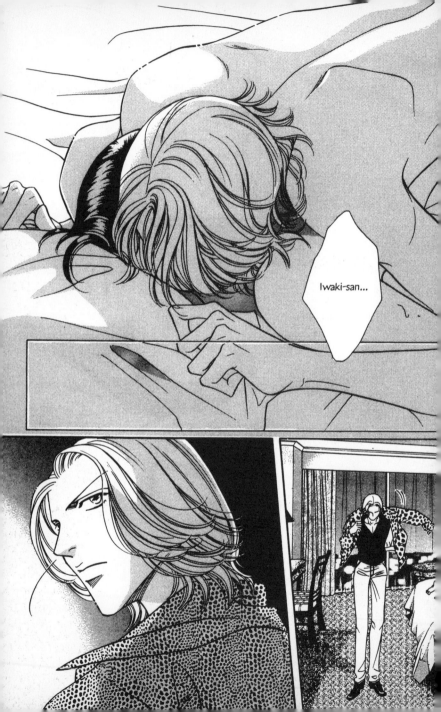

Iwaki-san...I have no intention of holding a press conference for such a stupid article.
But I'll be on a TV show the day after tomorrow, where I'm going to clear everything up.
I'd like for you to see it.
Come see the taping... okay?
...I'll be waiting...
SHUT

GLANCE
ちら
I Shinjuku 4:00
27
K TV Taping 14:00
...It's today.
RING
トゥルルル
RING
トゥルル
Do I dare show my face at the TV studio? It's not like I want to be **made** more of a laughing stock.
...Hello.
Is this Kyosuke Iwaki?
I don't recognize the voice...
If it's about the article, I have nothing to say.

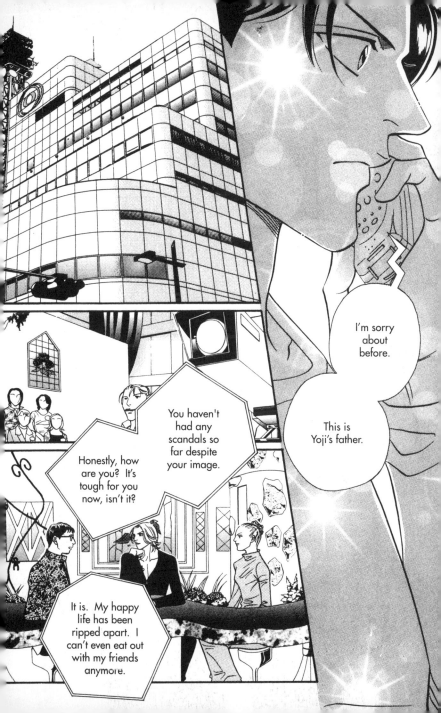

I'm sorry about before.

This is Yoji's father.

You haven't had any scandals so far despite your image.

Honestly, how are you? It's tough for you now, isn't it?

It is. My happy life has been ripped apart. I can't even eat out with my friends anymore.

What does Mr. Iwaki have to say about it?
He hasn't forgiven me. I'm really in a bind.
He won't even let me say what I want...
ちら
GLANCE
He didn't come after all...
We're in for a treat, folks. We have a letter from Mr. Katou's father!

What, for real?
Yes.
Dear son, I've only seen you on TV as of late, but I hope you're well.
You always did what you wanted, not worried about what others or your parents would think. You were easy to raise in that way.
Entering the adult film industry, becoming an actor, moving in with Iwaki—all these things you surprised me with **after** the fact.
I thought you couldn't surprise me anymore, but you did with this article.
Not because of the content, but because of how miserable you sounded when I received your call.
Normally you'd have laughed off something like this, but this time you were **serious.**

I'd like to cheer you up in person…
…But I know there's someone else you're rather see.
That's right, folks! We had planned to have Mr. Katou's father make an appearance, but by his request…
…We have Kyosuke Iwaki here, instead! Come in!
WOW!

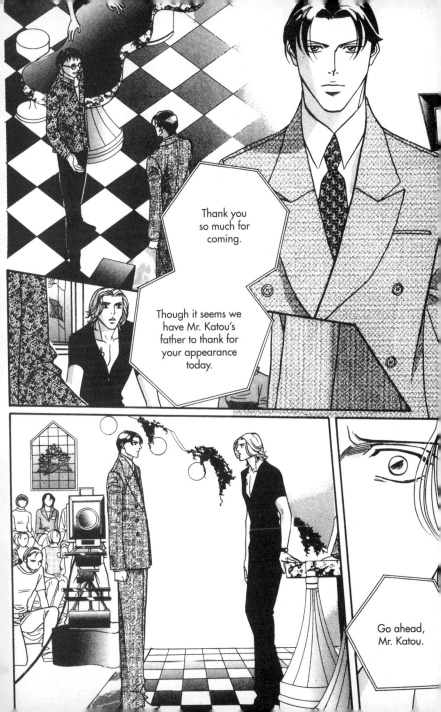

Thank you so much for coming.

Though it seems we have Mr. Katou's father to thank for your appearance today.

Go ahead, Mr. Katou.

Iwaki-san...
Your father lowered his head to me.
That's why I'm here.
You had something to say to me. I'm listening.

I...
I'm...
Sorry I made you cry...
PAT ぽん
...Stupid. **You're** the one that's crying.

But...
Katou's hands were shaking like a child's.
That, more than anything, made his suffering of the last few days painfully clear to me.

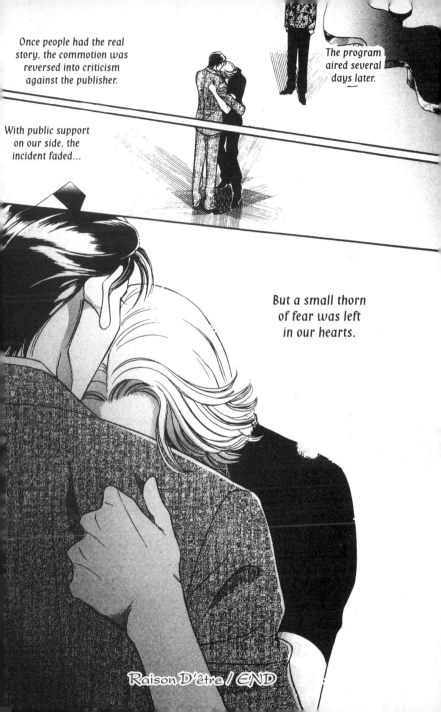

Once people had the real story, the commotion was reversed into criticism against the publisher.

The program aired several days later.

With public support on our side, the incident faded...

But a small thorn of fear was left in our hearts.

Raison D'être / END

Hey, Iwaki-san... We wanted to be top notch actors. Haven't we made it?
I hate to think back how many times we had to be cunning just to get by.
Outside of our work now, everything else is all the same...
...Second best.
So I work extra hard at this job.
If I can get the audience to watch a little longer.
I wouldn't hesitate taking off...
...Even the last piece of cloth.
NUDE DANCER

ヌードダンサー
NUDE DANCER

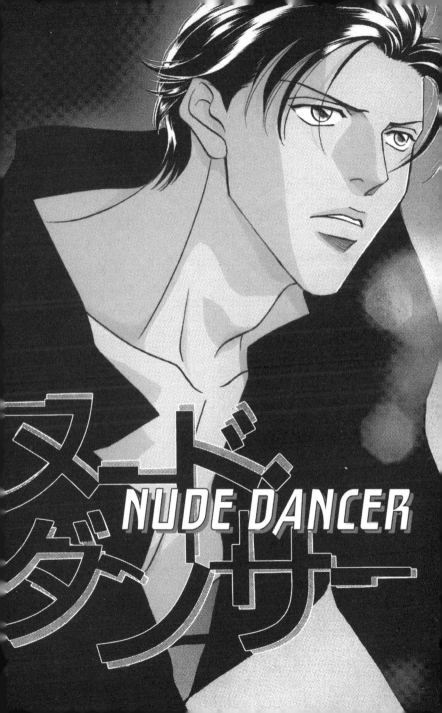

Y.KATOU
K.IWAKI

**EMBRACING
LOVE**

**Y.NITTA
PRESENTS**

That's right, folks! We had planned to have Mr. Katou's father make an appearance, but by his request...
...We have Kyosuke Iwaki here, instead! Come in!
WOW!

I'm sorry I made you cry...
Seems like the world of show business has **changed** since I've been gone.
It's as if they're calling for me...

Hurry up, Katou, or I'm leaving **without** you.
Hey, wait up! I thought we were going **together** for once.
I just got back from a photo shoot, you know.
RATTLE
It sure is rar your going a party...
You always have an excuse **not** to go.
STEP STEP
This party's being held to hype **your** new movie--you can't be late.
It's fine. It's really more for the sponsors, anyway.

STEP STEP
But I'm glad you're supporting me in my work.
Could it be you're coming to the party to **encourage** me?
SLIDE
You idiot, it's not like that!
Don't be ean on my big night!
could at least like, "Yeah! ood job!"
CLICK
Isn't your co-star, Kikuchi...
...Going to be there, tonight?
Katsuya Kikuchi?
Why, you like him?
You've never told me that.
Yeah, I've seen all his movies.
It was a shock when he left the business ten years ago because of that **same sex** scandal.

KA-KON
BEEP
Eventually he moved to America.
He was successful and earned a lot of respect there.
....
Stop...
I don't want you praising another guy in front of me.
...Idiot, cut it out!
FLASH
JUMP

Urushizaki !!
A great shot of the happily reunited couple.
You again. Cut it out already.
Who is this?
No one, really.
I approached him once because he looks like you, and now he gets carried away.
Though he oesn't look o much like you now.
aybe it's haircut.

He says he's a reporter, but he's really just an idol-chaser.
HMPH
Let's go.
Hey, wait!!
G-CHA
SHUT
Seeya later, Mr. Katou...
I'll be at the party tonight, too.

Be careful not to get caught by anyone else but me.
Since that last article was my doing, after all.
Stop playing around.
SHUT
VROOOM
BUMP
BUMP

Oh, it's Katou and Iwaki.
They're an impressive couple...on screen and off.

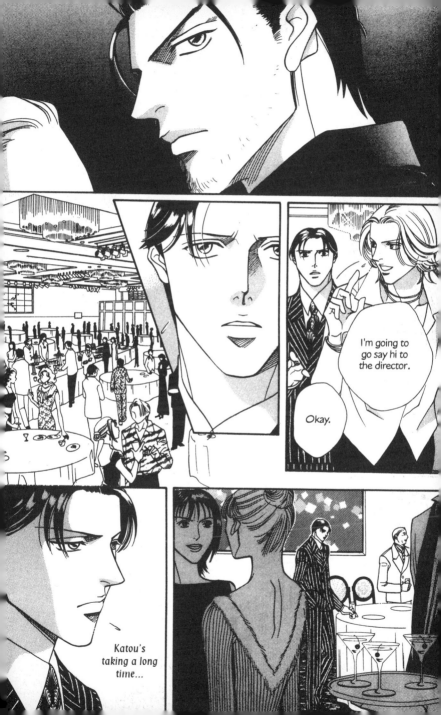

I'm going to go say hi to the director.

Okay.

Katou's taking a long time...

Are you Kyosuke Iwaki?
Ah...
Yes...
Ah, I thought so.
I'm glad. I really wanted to meet you.
I'll be co-starring with Katou.
...I know.

You're Katsuya Kikuchi. I'm a big fan...
I've seen all your movies...
Really? I'm glad.
But why did you want to meet me?
I'd seen several of Katou's videos.
When I accepted the offer for this movie...
...I was actually more interested in you, his co-star.
I thought you were a great actor.

That's... nice.
Would you like to go somewhere else with me?
Is there somewhere we can talk...
...in private?
Oh well...
...Where's Katou...
I'm going to get to see Katou every day from now on. I want to talk to **you**.
....
Whatever.
Katou left me alon here knowing tha I'm not very good at parties.
And this Kikuchi **seems** nice enough...
All right, let's go.

Maybe I'll introduce him when I get back.
This is the first time...
...that Iwaki's expressed interest in someone other than me.
Thinking that we could go the night without meeting Kikuchi...
...Was pretty **childish** of me.
I don't want to leave Iwaki alone for too long...
I should go back.
Huh? He's gone.

Iwaki-san!?

The New Otani
Hey, it's Kikichi and Iwaki!
Get a few words from them!
Kikuchi and Iwaki?
Strange...
Why isn't Katou with them?
They came here in Katou and Iwaki's car...
1650

I wonder what these two are doing together?
VROOOM

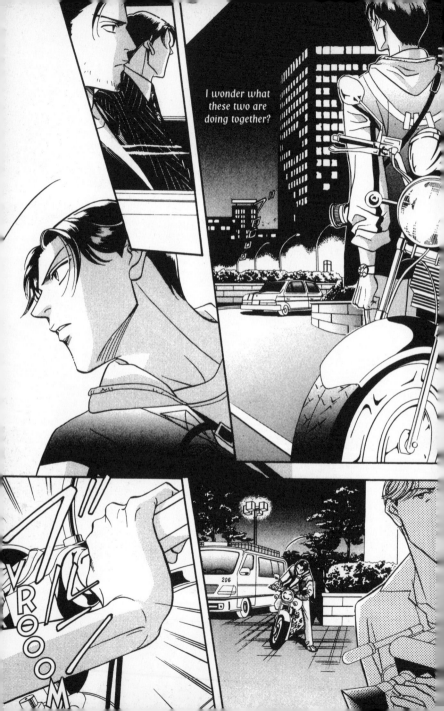

SCREECH

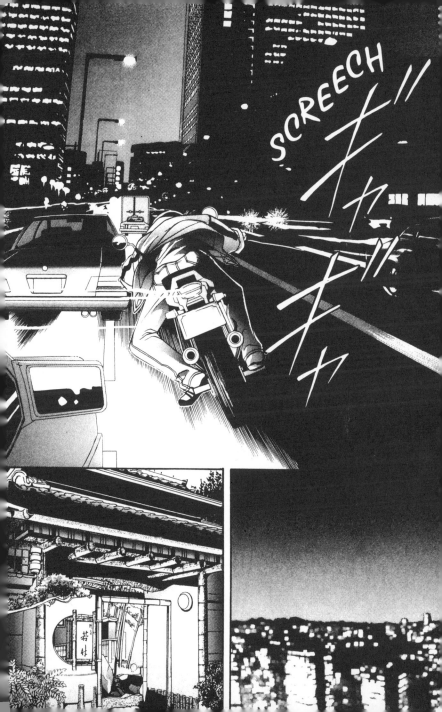

...As I was saying, being overseas made me want to eat some **real** food...like this.
Yeah.
BOW
Excuse me.
Thank you, that will be all.
After this we'll just drink saké, so don't worry about more food.
We'll call if anything's needed.

Iwaki.
HAH
Iwaki!?
You're barely here. Are you worried about leaving Katou at the party?
Excuse me?
After all, it's rather bad form to leave your lover to have dinner with another man.
No... I was just thinking I should have told him.
And he's not **really** my lover...

Coming back to Japan after so long was surprising.
I never imagined that a same sex couple like you two would be so **welcome** in Japan.
....
Do you know **why** I was forced out of the industry here?
I know a little...
In those days, being in a homosexual scandal was a fatal wound to an actor's career.
Things haven't changed much in ten years. The only reason **you're** accepted is because your relationship is marketed as "true love."
Katou's scandal is still fresh in people's minds. But if **you** were involved with

Your image as a **promiscuous** homosexual, that is.
The mainstream is **disgusted** by men who make love to other men.
It'd be a huge blow to both of you. But at least Katou would have the support of his female fanbase.
STAND
I don't like you two.
But I won't stir things up. I'm not trying to recreate myself.

You **disappoint** me by talking like that. I've always **admired** the way you lived.
Now that's a laugh! Are you saying you like me for the "way I live" rather than "who I am?"
Or would you rather think of me as a man who bravely struggled on despite the rumors of being gay?
WHAM
Urr...
Urnn...
No!!

Please stop it...!
Kikuchi!!
FLASH

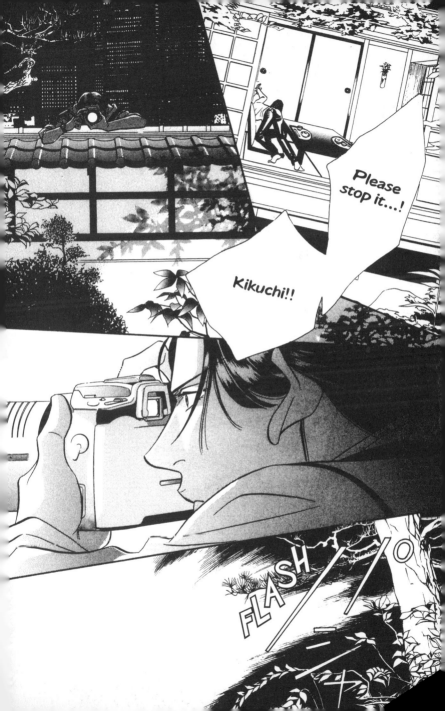

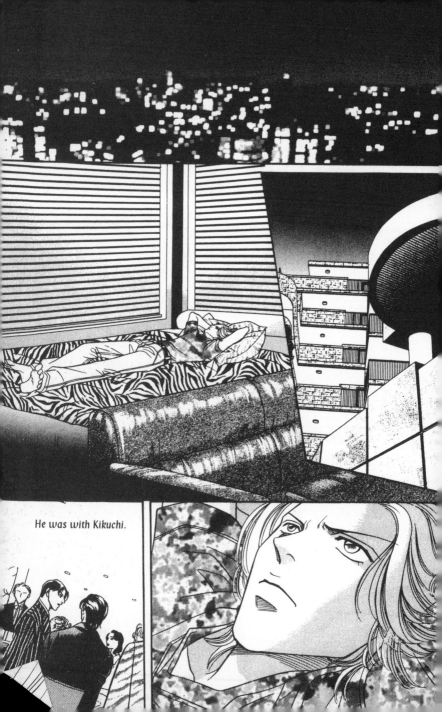

He was with Kikuchi.

I can't believe he's out this late with someone like that.
BITE
I doubt... Iwaki-san would...
SHUT
JUMP
FLINCH
Iwaki-san!!

Katou...
STEP
STEP
KACHA
Iwaki-san!! What happened?

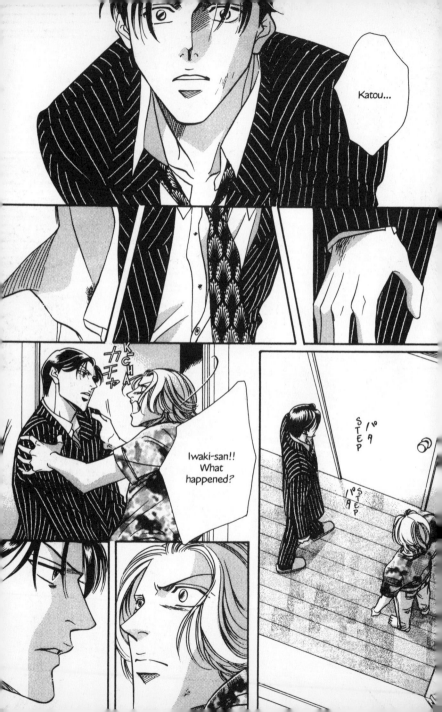

STARE
SLAP
SHUT

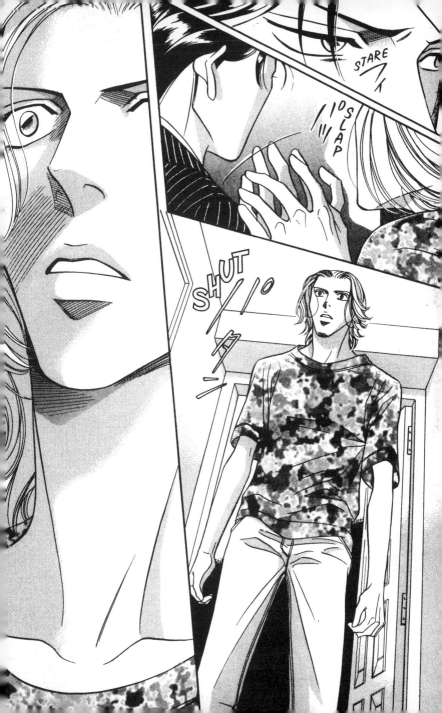

Why're your eyes so puffy, Mr. Katou?
VWOOOO
I'm sorry, I didn't sleep at all last night. Can you hide it with the makeup?
KNOCK
Awww, you TV stars have it ***soooo*** rough.
Were you waiting up last night for your mommy?

Shut up, you bastard! How dare you!?
SMAKK
EEKI!
Mr. Katou, what are you doing!? Please stop!
Get your hands off me, Kaneko!!

He forced himself on Iwaki-san!! And now he's gonna **pay**!!
...Forced?
Is that what he told you, Katou...
GRR
SMIRK
...Or what he wanted you to think? He told **me** you weren't really lovers.
The poor man feels positively **trapped** by your crazed, one-sided romance.
PAT PAT

Mr. Kikuchi, where are you going?
I'm going home. I already spoke to the director.
I'm not filming today. I just came to see the unprepared actor.
An actor who lets his lover's infidelity drive him to hit his co-star isn't very useful, is he?
Why don't you hurry home today and cry to your lover, maybe beg him to be faithful to you, huh?
Mr. Katou?
I'll show him...
Huh?

I'll show him that a man **crazed** by love...
...Can be a dangerous foe, indeed!
映画製作・企画
(有)共同企画
What!? Katou's leaving!?

What's going on!?
I don't know. He and Kikuchi had a big fight, and...
What the hell are you talking about!? We've already started filming!
SILENCE
Katou sure has a gotten a big head, for a new guy .
How dare he make us judge the value between him and Kikuchi.
Today's schedule is totally screwed... what a headache!
What'll we do, Director?
We can't **possibly** tell the sponsors!
...hmm...
WHAM
Director!!

This just came in by an anonymous courier!
RUSTLE
Huh?
RRING
RRING
What is this?
Kikuchi... and Iwaki...?
Oh my...
Yes!?
Is this Kyodo Kikaku Productions?
Have you seen the pictures?

Rumor has it...
...That Katou is asking for Kikuchi to back down?
...!! What are you talking about?
I'm sure he's angry with Kikuchi for laying his hands on his lover.
I wonder how the public will react when they hear about all this?
Hey, wait! Who are you--??
CLICK
Just a fan.

TBS
I'll bring the car around, Mr. Iwaki
1100
Hello, Iwaki-san.
What do **you** want? I thought it was Katou you were after?

Hm...I'm a little jealous.
ピク
FLINCH
About what?
I **really** shouldn't tell you, but it won't be good for **me** if Katou leaves show business.
Leave show business? What do you mean!?
You heard me. Katou's leaving his acting career...
...As **revenge** against Kikuchi.

SLAM
HAAAH
HAAAH
Welcome home. You're home early, Iwaki-san.

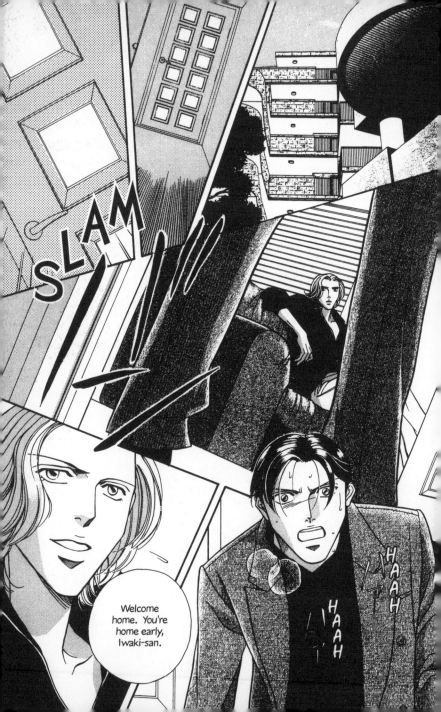

SLAP
I...I suppose that...you've already heard the big news. That was fast...

Who asked you to do that!?
This was your big chance...and you ruined it for yourself!!
Did you think that would make me **happy**!? Did you think that was what I **wanted**?!?
Fame is only **temporary** for people like us.
The industry is all-too quick to cast aside idiot actors that get big heads!
You **never** gave up on your dreams, Katou. Even when you were doing porn! And you finally made it.

If you lose work...and become forgotten...
...You'll never get another chance.
FLINCH
And if you sacrifice yourself like that...
Do you really think I can remain in this business?

...I'm sorry...
I'm **so** sorry, Iwaki-san...
But I can't stand it, anymore! We **did** do pornography...
...There isn't any part of our bodies that didn't end up on screen.
But all of those lovers meant nothing! The sex was meaningless! And...**I'd rather die...**
...Than let **anyone else touch you**!!

You're more important to me than the things I've wanted to do my entire life!
A fine performance, Katou...really great! But I'm not buying it! So quit acting like we're lovers!
Whaaat? **ME?!? You're** the one who's acting, Iwaki-san!!
If you didn't **care** about me, then you wouldn't have said all those things to encourage me!!

かく…
CRINGE
Stop it, Katou...
THUMP
PRADA
I can't stand you doing stupid things for me all the time.
I can't accept all of your feelings anymore. You are so dear to me...
...No.
Tell me, Iwaki-san.
Just say it!

Why!? Why can't you stand my being stupid!?
I've been stupid since the day that we first met!
And you're the only one that can fix my stupidity.
...It's because I like you... Katou...

FOOMP
I never thought I'd hear you say it. I could die happy... right now.
HEH
You'd die over something like this? You can't **ever** be serious.
I'm **completely** serious, Iwaki-san. I'm so happy, I don't care what happens tomorrow.
Let me make love to you, Iwaki-san.
Yeah.

FOOMP
Iwaki-san, you might not get too much sleep tonight.
Nn...
Mmm...

Your being aggressive is... pretty cool.
Idiot... Come over here.
Here I go, Iwaki-san.

Yes, Katou... deeper.
THAP
Aah!

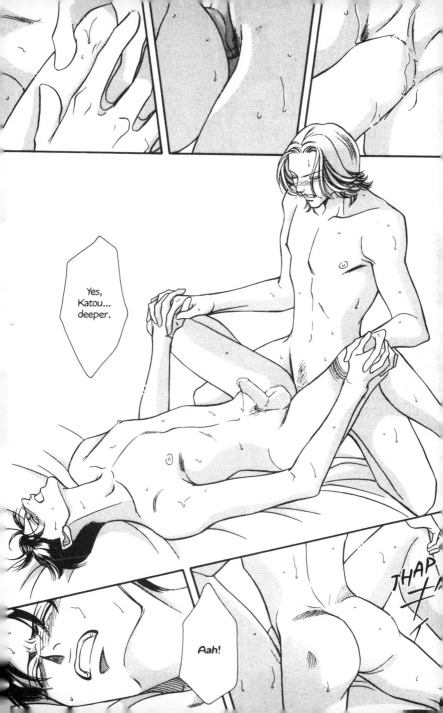

THAP
THAP
THAP
THAP

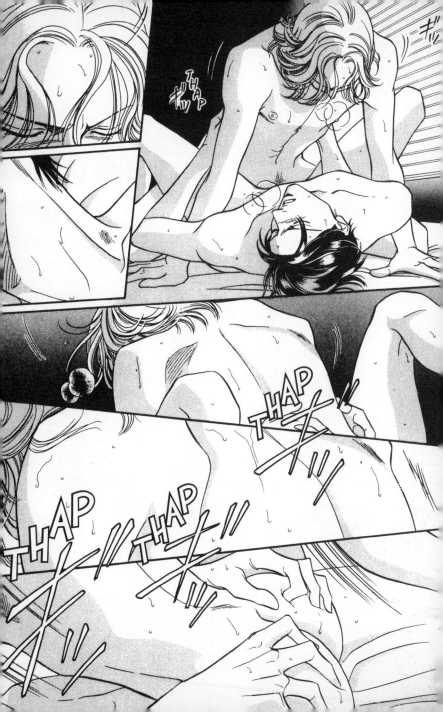

I'm gonna ...!!
HAAAH
HAAAH
That was great, Katou...
Yeah.

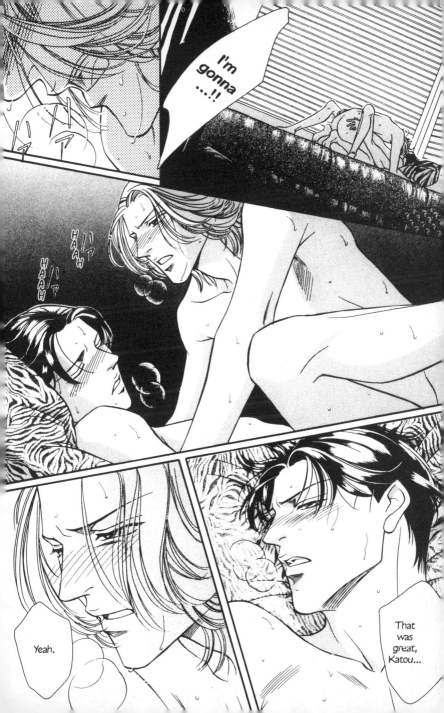

I love you.
I love you, Iwaki-san...
SQUEEZE
Yeah.
About yesterday...
....
No, nevermind.

Don't worry.
Kikuchi and I... We didn't go all the way.
STARTLE
Huh!?
I think it was hard on him, accepting us...
...when **he** hadn't been accepted, years before.
It's not like he was interested in me.
That's not it! I don't want anyone looking at you at all!
....

WHUMP
Now be quiet! I don't want to talk about anyone else right now!!
...Idiot. **You** brought it up, didn't you?

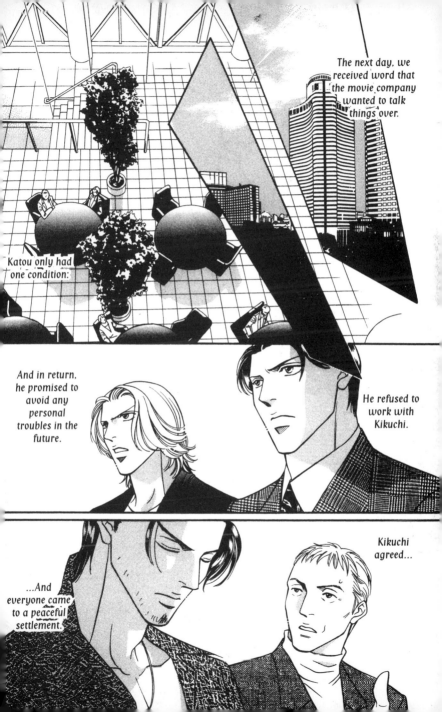

The next day, we received word that the movie company wanted to talk things over.

Katou only had one condition:

And in return, he promised to avoid any personal troubles in the future.

He refused to work with Kikuchi.

Kikuchi agreed...

...And everyone came to a peaceful settlement.

Looks like you owe me, Katou.

Huh?
STEP

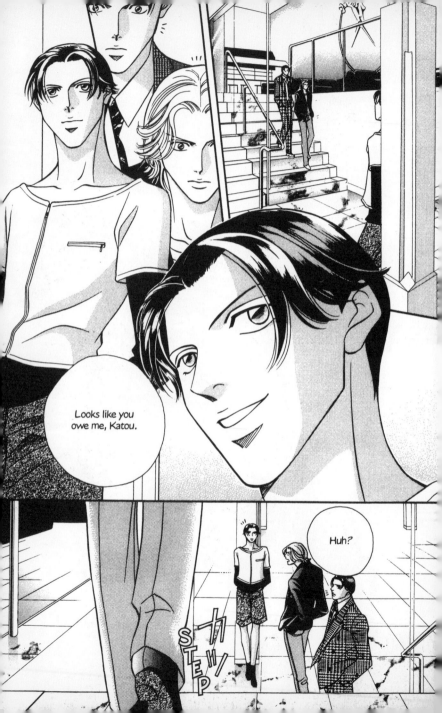

STEP
STEP
Japan really **has** changed. In **my** day, actors would **never** associate with their mortal enemy, the paparazzi.
Or maybe you're just trying to keep your career alive with another scandal, eh?
GLARE
HEH

Show business has changed, too.
Maybe I didn't have to run away ten years ago.
....
It's no use trying to get to Iwaki-san again.
He's with **me.** And **only** me.
HMMM
Wha!?
HEH
HA HA HA HA HA HA!!

Why's he laughing? The old man's pissing me off.
HA HA HA HA HA HA HA HA!
HUH?
He's just a sore loser, that's what!!
We're really lovers now, you tell him!
Your stupidity is totally incurable!!
MACK
HA HA HA HA HA HA HA HA!
Nude Dancer / END

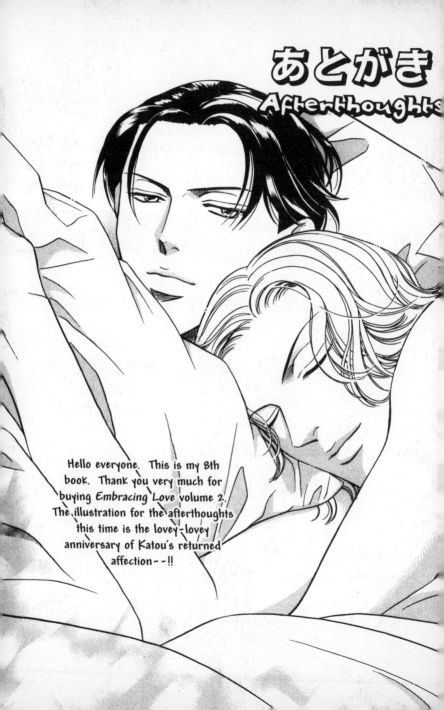

あとがき
Afterthoughts

Hello everyone. This is my 8th book. Thank you very much for buying *Embracing Love* volume 2. The illustration for the afterthoughts this time is the lovey-lovey anniversary of Katou's returned affection--!!

Well, hello there.
This is Youka Nitta.
And this is EB 2.
And I'm happy!

Yahoo!

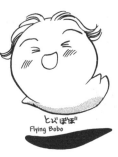

Lately, I've gotten a lot of letters of "What is a SaruBobo?" Let's see...A SaruBobo is a souvenir you can get from Hida, Takayama. It's very common.

とびぼぼ
Flying Bobo

←Like this

But I enjoy thinking up various themes for "Zips" and I always have 5 or 6 stories in stock, so I can never catch up.

I often get letters saying: "You'll run out of stories if you write at such a fast pace" or "Please don't get tired of writing this series and move on to another one."

Rejected comic cover sketch

In doing this series I always get very direct and helpful responses from the readers, and so continuing to draw Katou and Iwaki's story makes me very, very happy.

Thank you for your letters!

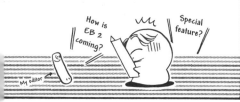

How is EB 2 coming?

Special feature?

My editor

My friend ⊗-chi says...

Maybe because Iwaki's so shy?

reserved...

So maybe his fans are shy, too?

ould that o...?

Though at the latest event, no one asked me to draw Iwaki for them.

Why were they all Katou...?

Now Iwaki is getting close to 8 times the number of letters as Katou.

Good luck, fans of Katou!

Speaking of which, when I mentioned in the last issue that Iwaki didn't have as many fans, I began to get many letters from fans.

Why not? I love Iwaki!!

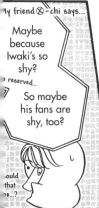

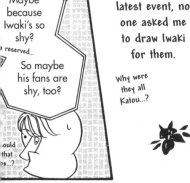

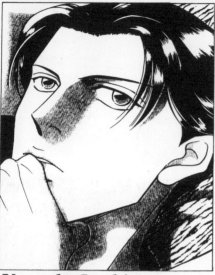

Kyosuke Iwaki

Born January 27th, 1970, in Niigata Prefecture.
An Aquarius. Blood type A. Height/Weight:
182 cm, 68 kg.

This time I decided to shed some light (cry) with the pair's profiles. (I meant to do it last time, but forgot).

Let's start with Iwaki, who lately has earned the nickname of 'maiden.' I'm often asked, will Iwaki no longer be the *"seme"? He will. In the future. On the other hand, there are many others whose opinion is he should "never be seme," but as it's vital to development of the story, please kindly continue to read. Next to that, I've been asked about how his voice should sound. I imagine him having a nice man's voice, like TERU, the vocalist for GLAY. I wonder if there will be a **drama CD, I keep waiting for the offer (laugh).

I did have a model for Iwaki, but since I don't think anyone knows who it is I'll keep it a secret. Please feel free to imagine.

*"seme" (roughly pronounced "say-may") is a term in the yaoi genre referring to the man who "tops" in a homosexual relationship.

**Embracing Love does have several drama CDs released under its Japanese title, "Haru wo Daiteita", starring well known voice actors Toshiyuki Morikawa as Iwaki and Shin'ichirou Miki as Katou.

• • • • • • • • • • • • • • • •

P E R S O N A L   D A T A

When Katou's family background became clear, I expected the question, "Why is his name *Yoji if he's the first born?" That's because his father's name is Yoichi. The Katou family has a lot of names starting in "Yo" (laughs).

Like Iwaki, for Katou's voice I imagine the mischievous voice of Siam Shade's Hideki.

And personally, I like many of their songs for Katou (or rather, for Embracing Love).

I'm keeping track of them on a separate paper. If you're interested, please send for them.

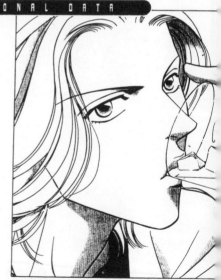

Yoji Katou

*The name "Yoji" includes the Japanese kanji for "two," which is usually given to a second born son. But because Katou's father, Yoichi, has "one" in his name, that makes Katou "Yo #2." His sister, similarly, is a "Yo" with a common girls' names suffix.

Born June 9th, 1975. Born in Chiba Prefecture. A Gemini. Blood type O. Height/Weight: 183 cm, 67 kg.

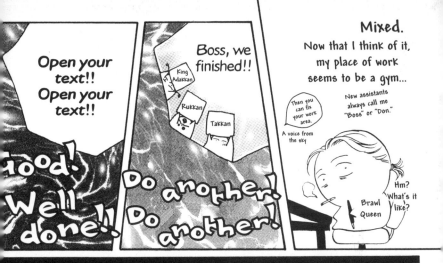

Open your text!! Open your text!!

Boss, we finished!!

King Adakkan

Rukkan

Takkan

Good! Well done!!

Do another! Do another!

Mixed.
Now that I think of it, my place of work seems to be a gym...

Then you can fix your work area.

A voice from the sky

New assistants always call me "Boss" or "Don."

Hm? What's it like?

Brawl Queen

Something like that...

It's not true...maybe one quarter.

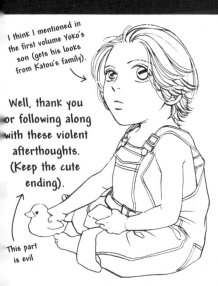

I think I mentioned in the first volume Yoko's son (gets his looks from Katou's family).

Well, thank you for following along with these violent afterthoughts. (Keep the cute ending).

This part is evil

Please continue to support the *Embracing Love* series.

Afterthoughts / END

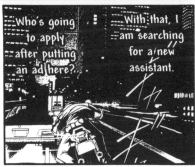

Who's going to apply after putting an ad here?

With that, I am searching for a new assistant.

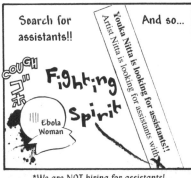

Search for assistants!!

And so...

Youka Nitta is looking for assistants!!
Artist Nitta is looking for assistants with

COUGH

Fighting Spirit

Ebola Woman

*We are NOT hiring for assistants!

COMING NEXT

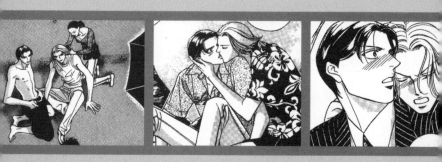

The romantic adventures continue as Iwaki and Katou engage in a ten da
sexual romp that leaves them exhausted, and eventually affects Iwaki
day job as an adult film star. But things take a turn for the worse whe
Iwaki finally confesses his love for Katou...a statement that the impossibl
beautiful blonde does not want to hear.

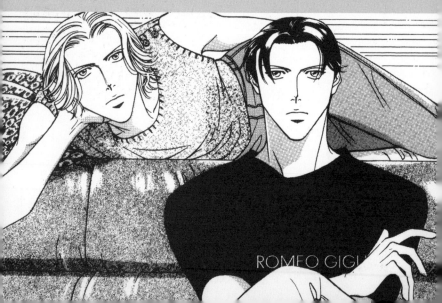

ROMEO GIGL

"A romantic epic" - The Village Voice
Kizuna
Bonds of Love
Story and art by Kazuma Kodaka
"A fantastic read... one tasty treat!" – SequentialTart.com
Volume 6 coming soon!
Volumes 1-5 available now!
To order, call: 1-800-626-4277 or visit BeBeautifulManga.com
Warning: These graphic novels may contain violence, nudity, and sexual situations. Reader discretion advised. Be Beautiful graphic novels are absolutely not for readers under 18 years of age. All characters depicted in sexual conduct or in the nude are aged 19 years or older. No actual or identifiable minor was used in the creation of any character depicted herein. Ad layout & copy ©2005 A18 Corporation. Original Japanese version "Kizuna Vol. 4" © 1998 Kazuma Kodaka. Originally published in Japan in 1999 by BIBLOS Co., Ltd. Be Beautiful, Original Yaoi and logos are trademarks of A18 Corporation. All rights reserved.
Original 愛 Yaoi

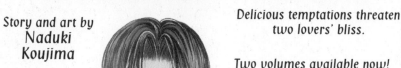

Selfish Love

Story and art by
**Naduki
Koujima**

*Delicious temptations threaten
two lovers' bliss.*

Two volumes available now!

*Book 1 includes
four extra bonus
stories!*

To order, call: 1-800-626-4277 or visit BeBeautifulManga.com

FINDER SERIES 1:
TARGET in the FINDER

When valuable information falls into the hands of a freelance photographer, the Chinese mafia will go to extreme measures to take it back from him.

tory and art by
yano Yamane

To order, call: 1-800-626-4277 or visit BeBeautifulManga.com

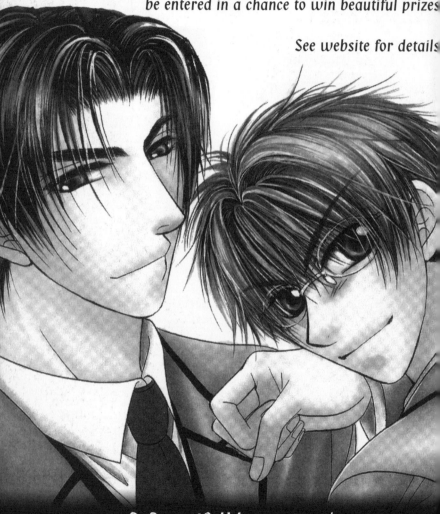

Dear Friend

We want to find out more about you and your thoughts on our Be Beautiful graphic novels. Please visit our online survey and be entered in a chance to win beautiful prizes.

See website for details

www.BeBeautifulManga.com/survey

This sign reads "Tomare" and it means:

STOP!

THIS IS THE LAST PAGE
OF THE BOOK! DON'T
RUIN THE ENDING
FOR YOURSELF.
This book is printed in the
original Japanese format,
which means that it reads
from right to left
(example on right).

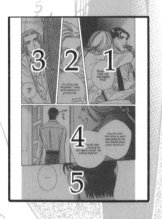

You'll find that all Original Yaoi books that are part of our
Be Beautiful line are published in this format. The original
artwork and sound effects are presented just like they were in
Japan so you can enjoy the comic the way the creators intended.

This format was chosen by YOU, the fans. We conducted a
survey and found that the overwhelming majority of fans prefer
their manga in this format.

The ideogram in the Be Beautiful logo
is pronounced as "Be" in Japanese.
It means "beauty" or "aestheticism".

The ideogram in the Original Yaoi
logo is pronounced as "Ai" in
Japanese. It means "love".